# THE OFFICIAL
# F·R·I·E·N·D·S
## THE TELEVISION SERIES
# COLORING BOOK

**SCHOLASTIC INC.**

Compiled by Micol Ostow
Illustrated by Keiron Ward

All rights reserved. Published by Scholastic Inc., *Publishers since 1920.*
SCHOLASTIC and associated logos are trademarks and/or registered trademarks of Scholastic Inc.

The publisher does not have any control over and does not assume any responsibility for author or third-party websites or their content.

This book is a work of fiction. Names, characters, places, and incidents are either the product of the author's imagination or are used fictitiously, and any resemblance to actual persons, living or dead, business establishments, events, or locales is entirely coincidental.

ISBN 978-1-338-79090-0

10 9 8 7 6 5 4 3 2 1     21 22 23 24 25

Printed in the U.S.A.   40

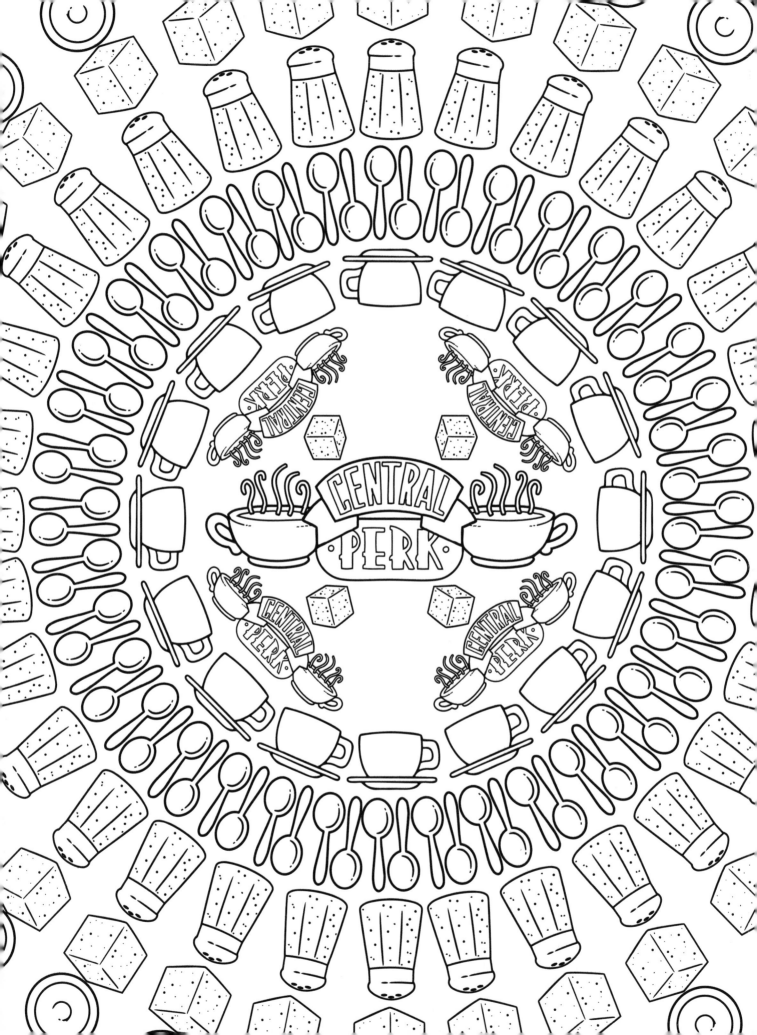

# HAPPY HOLIDAYS!

# LONDON, BABY!

# WHAT IF I DON'T WANT TO BE A SHOE?

F·R·I·E·N·D·S

CENTRAL PERK

A MOOOVINGLY RICH AND CREAMY COFFEE STRAIGHT FROM THE MUTTER'S UTTER

LOADED WITH CAFFEINE WE DON'T RECOMMEND DOING NEEDLEPOINT AFTER A CUP OF THIS JOE

GOING SHOPPING YOU'LL NEED SOME FUEL, TRY THIS TRENDY BLEND WHILE YOU SPEND

BURSTING WITH FLAVOR & ENERGY, YOU WON'T BE HANGING AROUND AFTER DRINKING THIS STUFF

A LIBERATING BLEND, LIGHT & SWEET! YOU'LL BE CRYING "FREEDOM"! WHEN YOU TASTE IT

THE CLASSIC COFFEE TASTE YOU'D EXPECT ON A CLASSIC NEW YORK MORNING

FILTERED THROUGH THE FINEST SKID ROW HANKIES! WE GET A BREW SO THIN YOU'D THINK IT'S TEA

A STIMULATING BREW GUARANTEED TO KEEP YOUR EYES OPEN!

A SYMPHONY OF FLAVORS BLENDED TOGETHER TO MAKE YOUR DAY SING

ROBUST AND RAW, THIS COFFEE WILL HAVE YOU SWINGING FROM THE LAMPOSTS

# THE MEANING OF THE BOX IS THREEFOLD

doin'?

# THEY DON'T KNOW THAT WE KNOW THEY KNOW WE KNOW

# MONICA

I AM ALWAYS THE HOSTESS

# WHAT GETS OUT HUMMUS?

# LAUNDRY DAY

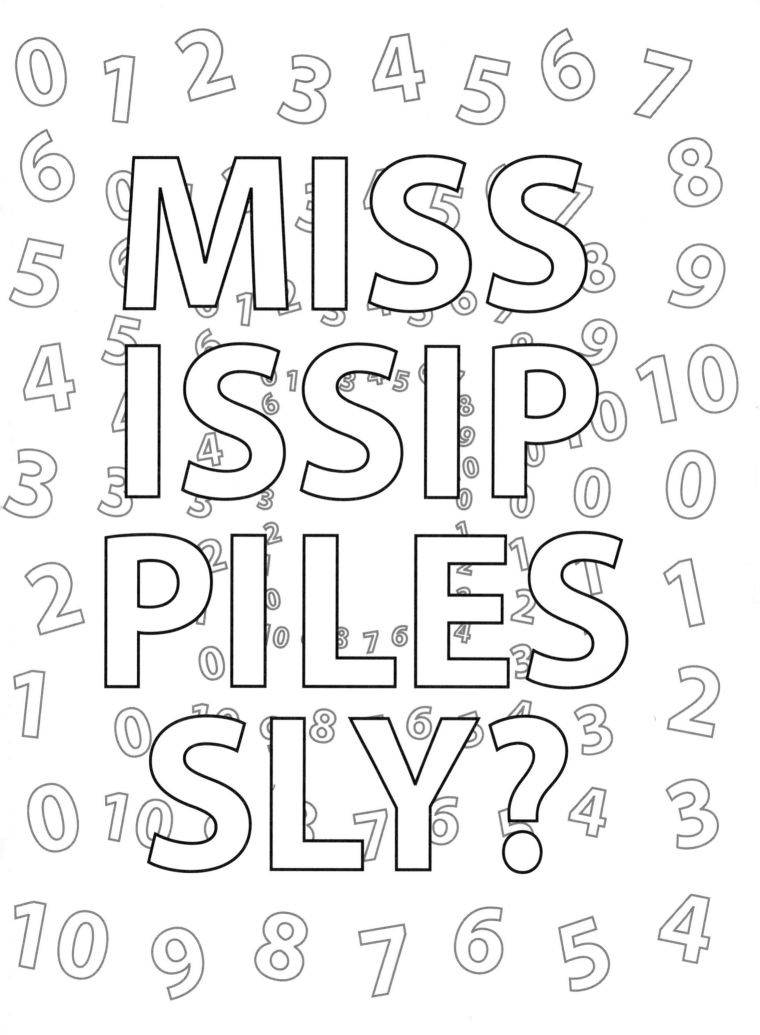

# MONICA'S SECRET CLOSET

# MMM... NOODLE SOUP

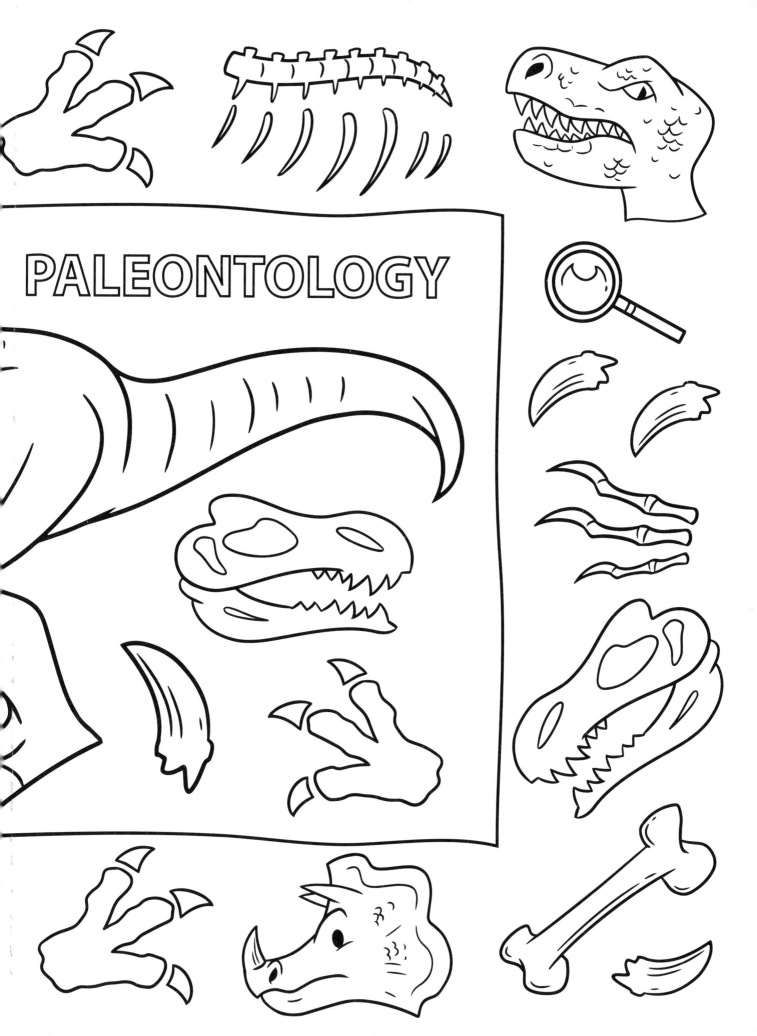

PALEONTOLOGY

# GRAB A SPOON

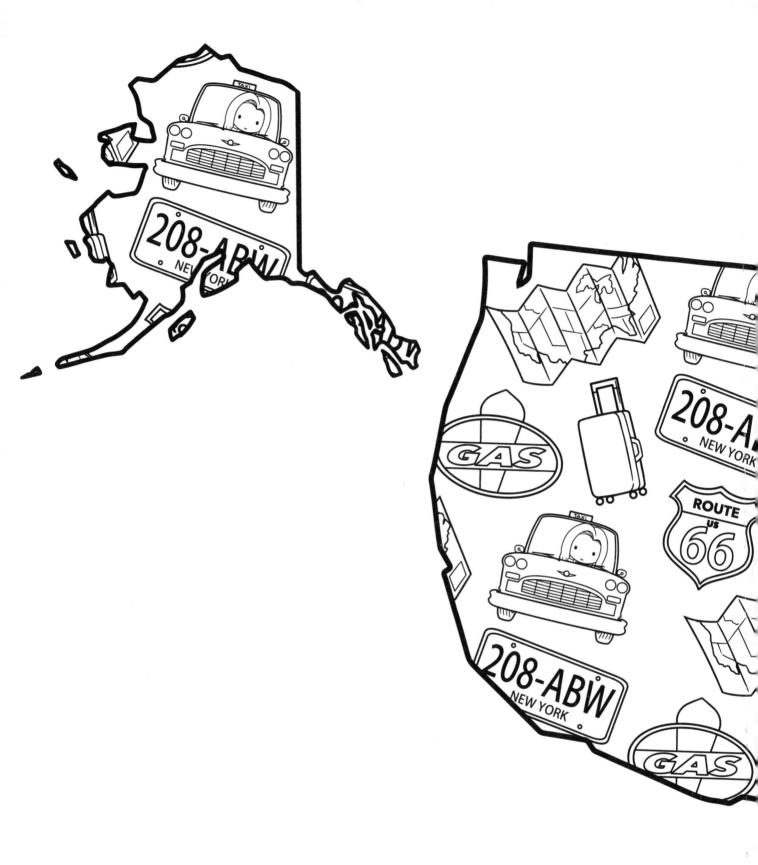

# Joey's Days of the Week

MONDAY: One day

TUESDAY: Two day

WEDNESDAY: When? what day?

THURSDAY: The third day

FRIDAY:

SATURDAY:

SUNDAY: